My Book of
Fables

 STERLING

Contents

The Ant and the Grasshopper

A silly young grasshopper did nothing but play in the spring and laze around during the warm sunny months of summer. It did not think of working to save food for the cold winter months.

Soon winter arrived and it had nothing to eat. It was dying of hunger.

At last it went to its neighbour, a hardworking ant. It knocked at the door.

The ant opened the door and heard the grasshopper's plea. But it felt no pity for the

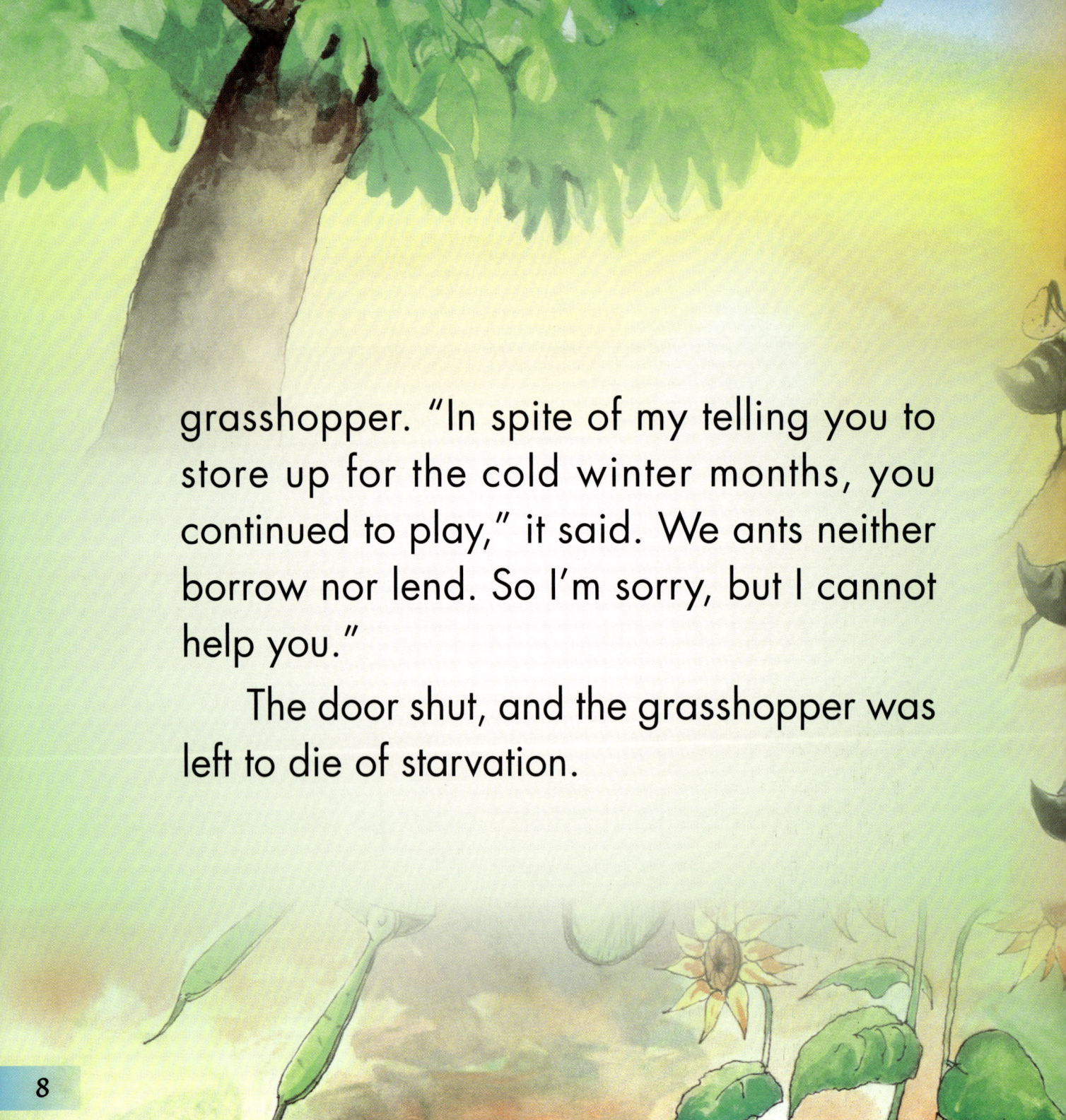

grasshopper. "In spite of my telling you to store up for the cold winter months, you continued to play," it said. We ants neither borrow nor lend. So I'm sorry, but I cannot help you."

The door shut, and the grasshopper was left to die of starvation.

It is wise to save up for a rainy day.

9

The *Old Man* and the *Donkey*

An old man and his son were off to the market to sell an donkey. They walked along beside the donkey.

A passer-by commented, "How foolish can you get! Instead of riding the ass, why do you walk?" At this, the old man lifted his son onto the donkey.

A little further, another traveller said to the boy, "You little rascal! How can you ride the donkey while your father trudges along!"

Ashamed of himself, the son made his father sit on the donkey.

11

Then they came across a third person who was shocked that the old man was riding the donkey while his small son walked.

The father got fed up. They tied the donkey's legs to a log and carried it on their shoulders. This amused everyone. Humiliated at being laughed at, the old man threw the donkey into the river and went home. Another man who saw this saved the donkey and took it home.

It is foolish to change your way of thinking each time someone expresses an opinion.

The *Wind* and the **Sun**

One day the wind and the sun had an argument. Each claimed itself stronger of the two. They agreed to have a contest. Whichever of them made a traveller take off his coat first would be considered the stronger one.

The wind was the first to try and make the traveller remove his coat. It blew and it blew and it blew with great fury. But the more it blew, the more tightly did the traveller clutch his coat. No matter how hard the wind tried, it remained unsuccessful.

Then it was the sun's turn to make the traveller remove his coat. At first it shone gently and drove away the chill that the wind had created. Then it grew brighter and brighter and therefore warmer and warmer, till it was so hot that the traveller had to remove his coat to be at ease.

The sun had won without force or fury. It had persuaded the traveller gently.

Gentleness and warmth are better ways of persuasion than force.

The Raven and the Swan

Once upon a time there lived a raven, who was unhappy because of its black colour. It envied a swan for its whiteness.

"How pretty it looks! So white and clean! Perhaps it's because it is always washing itself in the lake," thought the raven. "I wish I could wash off my black colour too."

Near the raven's home there was a big lake. All kinds of birds played and preened themselves in this pool.

The raven decided to bathe in the lake. "Doing the same will, perhaps, make me as white and as beautiful as the swan," it said. It bathed and it bathed and it bathed, but it saw no change in its complexion. It remained as black as it was, and also as discontent.

A content person is a happy one.

Two Cats and some Cheese

Two cats found a piece of cheese. They cut it into two pieces. But one piece was slightly bigger. Each cat wanted the piece which was bigger. So they went to a monkey and asked it to solve their problem.

"Don't worry," said the monkey to the cats, "I will soon make both the pieces equal." Saying this, it ate a bit from the piece that was bigger. But one piece was still bigger than the other. So again it bit off a part of the bigger piece. When it looked at the pieces, they were still not equal. This continued till the pieces were reduced to very small sizes.

The cats seeing this pleaded, "Please, Your Majesty, we are satisfied. Let us have the pieces now."

The cunning monkey replied, "But the remaining pieces are so small. This is my fee for sorting out your problem." And saying this, it gobbled up the remaining cheese.

It is better to settle quarrels quickly and peacefully, otherwise someone else will take advantage of you.

A Snake and a Knife

Once upon a time, a snake got into an interesting-looking shop. This shop sold all kinds of knives. There were hunting knives, carving knives, kitchen knives and table knives. The knives looked very attractive. Their blades glittered in the light and their wooden handles were well polished.

The snake started licking one of the knives. Very soon, it saw blood on the knife. Being cruel by nature, it licked harder and harder. The snake

was quite glad that it was hurting the knife. The more blood it saw, the happier it became. Little did the foolish snake know that it was its own tongue that was bleeding.

After quite some time, it started feeling tired and faint and before it knew what was happening, it fell down unconscious.

If we rejoice in harming others, we may end up harming ourselves.

A **Fox** and a **Raven**

A raven sat on a tree with a morsel of food in its mouth. A hungry fox sat beneath the tree. Its mouth was watering for that morsel. It thought hard about how to get that bit of food.

"O beautiful bird," it said, "you are so graceful and good-looking. You are a delight to anyone who sees you. If you have a voice as beautiful as your looks, there will not be a creature in the world to match you."

This flattery did the trick. The raven started singing to display its beautiful voice. As it opened its beak wide to entertain the fox, the morsel of food fell out of its mouth, into the open mouth of the fox standing below.

"Though I praised your beauty," laughed the fox, "I said nothing about your brain!" So saying, the fox went his way.

Never be deceived by flattery.

The *Frogs Want* a *Ruler*

A long time ago there lived some frogs in a pond. All the time they argued with each other and so they wanted a ruler who would end their disputes.

The gods sent them a ruler in the form of a log. It splashed into the water and frightened all the frogs. But as the log stayed still, they realised that it was harmless and started taking advantage of it. They found this ruler unsatisfactory and so they asked the gods for another one. This time they were sent a snake which gave them no freedom at all. In fact, it made a prey of all the frogs and so that was the end of them and their arguments.

Men realise the worth of a kind
ruler only when a tyrant rules them.

29

A **Horse** and a **Stag**

A wild horse was grazing on a grassland which it had all to itself. After a while it saw a stag come and nibble on the same grassland. The horse did not like sharing the grass and so it wanted to get rid of the stag.

As it stood wondering about how to do this, it saw a man pass by. It told the man about its plan and asked him if he would help it kill the stag. The man agreed, but said that to achieve this, he would have to bridle the horse and mount

it in order to chase the stag. The horse submitted to this and very soon the man killed the stag. But once he had done this, he refused to alight from the horse's back, saying that the horse would have to become his beast of burden.

The horse was mad with rage and began to kick and fling, but all it got was a good whipping. It finally had to submit to the man and was harnessed for labour on a farm.

Sharing is good. It also wins you friends.

The Two Buckets

Two buckets, tired after a day's work, sat down to rest.

One of the buckets was always grumbling. It never looked at life cheerfully.

As it rested outside the well it said to the other bucket, "I'm tired of the life we lead. However full we are when we are drawn up out of the well, we are sent back empty again. This makes me very dissatisfied."

The second bucket was of a different nature. It did not believe in grumbling. It always looked at life positively. It said, "That's true. But I always look at it this way – that however empty we are when we are sent down, we are always full when drawn up."

It is good to look on the brighter side of life.

The Lion in Love

A lion was in love with a farmer's beautiful daughter. He asked her father for her hand in marriage. The poor frightened farmer did not like it at all. He thought hard about how to avoid this match.

Finally, he struck upon an idea. "My daughter," said he to the lion, "is a foolish, frightened girl. Perhaps if you have your

teeth removed and your nails pared, she may agree to marry you."

The lion agreed and went to a dentist to have his teeth pulled out. Next he got his nails pared. As soon as the task was over, he went to claim his bride. But the clever farmer, armed with a cudgel, struck him down dead, thus bringing the match to an end.

Physical strength may be overcome by intelligence.

The Boot in the Jungle

Deep in the jungle where no man went, there lived many a wild beast. One day they came across a strange object. It was a man's boot. They had never seen a thing like it before.

"I am sure it's the shell of a fruit," said the bear.

"Rubbish!" said the wolf. "Can't you see that it's a nest? Here is the hollow in which the bird lays its eggs."

"How can you be so foolish!" said the goat pointing to the long laces. "Look here, these are roots. So obviously it is a plant."

A duck was listening to their argument. It said, "I have been to a land where many men live and this thing you see is called a boot. Men wear such things on their feet."

"You keep out of this," said the quarrelsome bear. "What you say can't be true. We have seen no such thing and so we can't believe you."

"Believe what you want to, but remember that you can't know everything."

Many things that you cannot see do exist in the world.

The Discontented Dog

A dog had just finished its lunch and was lazing in the garden, when it saw a cat on top of a high wall. "It must feel so nice to be high above the ground. If only I could climb!" it thought. This feeling of envy made it so bad-tempered, that it would not even wag its tail at its master who came to give it some milk.

It next saw some goldfish in the aquarium and wished that it too could live in water. The water would keep it cool, it thought. Envy made it angry once again. Just then it heard the fish

43

say: "It looks so nice and warm on the grass. I wish I too could lie down on it."

Shortly a sparrow flew past. Seeing the dog lazing around, it said aloud: "I wish I could play all day long like this dog. I wish I didn't have to build myself a house, search for food and tire my wings."

Listening to all of them the dog realised how foolish it was in not appreciating what it had.

The grass is always greener on the other side.

An *Honest* *Woodcutter*

A poor woodcutter accidentally dropped his axe into a river. He was very upset because he had no money to buy another axe.

As he stood by the river, feeling very sad and not knowing what to do, a fairy appeared. She stood in the river holding out a golden axe to him.

"Perhaps this is your axe. I found it in the river," she said.

"That's not mine," said the woodcutter.

The fairy then brought out a silver axe. The

woodcutter disowned this one too. Finally, the fairy held out an axe with a wooden handle.

"That's mine," said the woodcutter, smiling with happiness. "Thank you for getting my axe back for me!"

"Such honesty deserves a reward," said the fairy and she gave the poor man all the three axes.

Honesty is the best policy.

The Hare and the Tortoise

Said the hare to the tortoise, "What a slow and heavy creature you are! I am sure I can defeat you in a race."

"I am slow and heavy, it is true, and yet I'll run a race with you," replied the tortoise.

Some other animals present agreed to judge the race and soon it was flagged off. The hare was excited. It knew that it was as swift as the wind. It would surely win. With a song in its heart it ran and it ran, till it reached the mid-point of the racetrack. "I've got plenty of time," it thought.

FINISH

49

"The tortoise is far behind."
And so it lay down to take a
nap.

Meanwhile the tortoise
trudged along. Always keeping
its goal in mind, it never paused
to take a break. And as it
laboured along patiently, it
passed the sleeping hare and
finally reached the winning
post before the hare.

Slow and steady wins the race.

An Ant and a Pigeon

It was a hot summer afternoon. A tiny, thirsty ant was drinking water from a brook. It suddenly slipped and fell into the water. The poor little creature did all it could to get back on to dry land, but in vain. Each time it slipped back into the brook.

A pigeon flying by saw this unfortunate incident. It took pity on the ant. The pigeon tried to help the ant. It handed the ant a twig, onto which it climbed and saved itself.

It so happened that a few days later the ant saw a hunter taking aim at the very same pigeon. It recalled how the pigeon had saved its life. Without losing time, it went up to the hunter and bit him really hard. The hunter lost his aim and the pigeon flew away to safety.

One good turn deserves another.

53

A Wolf and a Crane

A greedy wolf was gobbling down its meal. It was stuffing itself so quickly that it got a bone stuck in its throat. The wolf was in great discomfort. It wondered what to do. Just then it saw a crane passing by. It pleaded with the crane to remove the bone.

"Please save me! You alone can help me with your long beak," it begged. "And if you do so, I shall reward you well for it," it said, almost choking.

The crane agreed to help the wolf. Then having done the good deed it demanded its reward. But the ungrateful, cunning wolf changed its tune by telling the crane that it was lucky that its head had not been bitten off. The wolf said that sparing its head was reward enough.

Expect no reward for a kind deed done.

A *Lion* and a *Mouse*

A mouse once ran over the body of a sleeping lion. The lion woke up and caught the mouse.

"You're a nice morsel before dinner, my precious," it said.

The mouse, trembling with fear, begged for forgiveness. "I promise to repay you for your kindness if you spare me," said the mouse.

"Repay me!" laughed the lion. "That's rather far-fetched, little one! All the same, I'll let you go."

A few days later as the mouse scampered through the forest, it heard a lion groan. As it went closer, the mouse saw that it was the same lion which had captured it a few days ago. Some hunters had trapped the lion in a net and had tied it to a tree.

"You laughed at me when I promised to repay your kindness," said the mouse. "Now is my chance to be true to what I said." The mouse then started gnawing at the rope and soon set the lion free.

A kind deed is always repaid.

Grapes are Sour

Once upon a time there was a fox who was different from its clan. While all other foxes craved for a leg of mutton, this fox would do anything for a bunch of grapes.

As it walked along, it came across a delicious-looking cluster hanging from a vine. But it hung on a wall, just a little beyond its reach. It stood licking its lips and gazing longingly at the grapes, wondering how to get them. Then it started jumping towards them, but in vain.

Soon the fox started getting agitated. It jumped and it jumped, each time a bit higher. A hare passing by cheered it on. But the encouragement could not help it reach the grapes.

"Forget them," it said. "I am sure they are sour!" And swallowing its disappointment, it went its way.

It is good to accept defeat sportingly.

The Ox and the Frog

An ox was grazing in a meadow. A frog in a pond nearby saw the ox and found it huge and majestic. The frog started envying the ox. It said to itself, "What a big creature this is! I wish I too could be as huge!" Saying this, it breathed deep to swell its body to the size of the ox. It breathed deeper and deeper, stopping time and again to check if it had reached the same size. It obviously had not. Getting annoyed at the slow progress, it breathed deeper and faster, till it puffed itself up so much, that it finally burst.

We should be happy with what we are and not try to copy others. Or else, we might have to pay a dear price for it, like the envious frog.

It is foolish to try to make ourselves appear greater than we are.

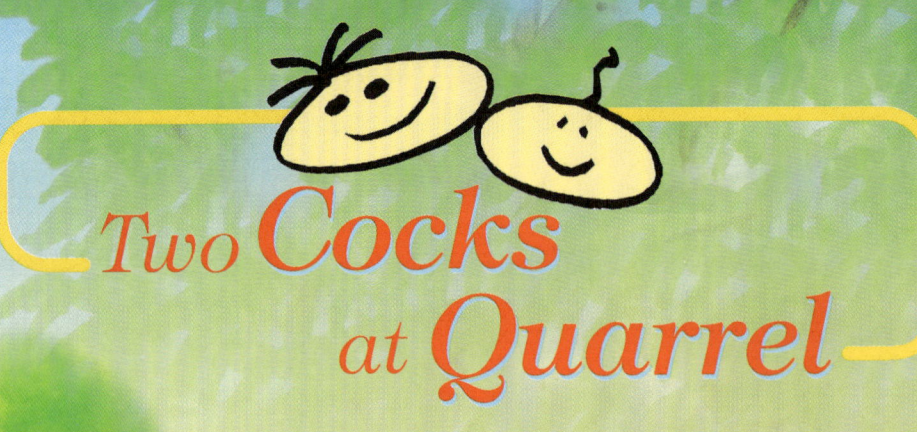

Two Cocks at Quarrel

Once there lived two cocks in a farmer's backyard "There can only be one master in this yard," said one cock to the other. "To prove who is the leader, let us have a duel." The other agreed to this.

Soon the hen yard was full of noise, dust and anger. The cocks fought, striking and pecking at each other. There were feathers flying everywhere, and the hens and chicks fled away in terror.

Not much later the duel was over. The defeated cock was scared and ashamed. The victor flew to the top of the house, and crowed and clapped its wings in victory and made great fun of the loser. It made such a show of its triumph, that an eagle flying by noticed it and swooped down and carried the victorious cock away. Then the cock who had been defeated had the yard to itself.

Making fun of the defeated is unwise, because fortune always changes.

The Thirsty Crow

"Oh what a hot day it is! And not a drop of water in sight!" said a thirsty crow. It flew from place to place looking for some water. But all the lakes and rivers had dried up and there was no sign of rain.

"I'll surely die of thirst," said the crow.

As it searched here and there in desperation, it spotted a large container in front of a deserted house. It perched on it and saw that there was some water at the bottom, beyond reach.

It thought hard and soon an idea came to its mind. There were many pebbles lying nearby. It picked up the pebbles one by one, and dropped them into the container. Slowly the water level started rising. The crow kept at it, never giving up. Soon the water level was high enough for it to reach and it was able to quench its thirst.

Where there is a will there is a way.

The Dog and the Bone

A dog sat chewing at a delicious bone that it had found near the river. It chewed the bone for a very long time and soon this made it quite thirsty. It decided to go to the river to quench its thirst. It took the bone along as it was worried that some other dog might take it away.

As it stood near the river, the dog looked around to see if it was safe to put the bone down while it quenched its thirst. It saw its reflection in the water. It thought it was another dog with

a bone in its mouth. And being greedy by nature, it wanted that bone too. So it barked at the other dog, hoping to scare it into giving it that bone. But alas! The bone that it held in its mouth fell into the river.

Foolish dog! Little did it realise that it was its own reflection that it was looking at.

Greed can lead to foolishness.

Two Burdened Asses

Two asses trudged along, quite weary under their heavy loads. One ass was laden with salt and the other with cotton. As they were crossing a river, the ass laden with salt stumbled and fell down in the river. When it got up, it seemed to be walking more easily than before. Seeing this, the ass carrying the cotton thought that it should do the same thing. It sat down in the river, and then got up hoping that its burden would be lighter and its journey easier.

But it was unlucky. In the case of the first ass the water had dissolved the salt and therefore its burden had become lighter. But in the case of the second ass the cotton soaked up the water, and its burden became many times heavier. The poor ass nearly drowned under the added weight!

Imitation without intelligence is foolish.

The Foolish Goats

A goat decided to taste the grass on the other side of a narrow log bridge. It came face to face with another goat that was coming from the other side. Only one animal could cross at a time.

"Let me pass," said the first goat to the other.

"You let me pass first," snapped back the other.

They started fighting so savagely that losing their balance they fell into the stream below.

The other goats grazing on the hills saw this spectacle and learnt a lesson.

On another occasion two other goats were faced with the same problem.

"I'll sit down and you can step over my body," said one goat to the other.

"Thank you. That's very kind of you," said the other goat. "Next time, I'll sit down and let you across first."

Thus they were able to cross the bridge safely.

Problems cannot be solved through violence.

A Bear and some Bees

It was a lazy summer afternoon.

A bear was sleeping peacefully beneath a big, leafy tree. Just then a bee passing by saw it. The bee decided to sting the bear. Enraged at this, the bear went mad and decided to get back at the bees. It charged towards the beehive and knocked down all of them in revenge.

Now it was the turn of the bees to get angry. They were so wild that they could not bear this insult. They decided to take revenge and punish the bear. The bees swarmed towards the bear to teach it a lesson. As a result, the bear got badly stung. Later it said to itself, "It would have been wiser for me to let one injury pass than to receive so many."

How true it was. The bear would have been better off with one bee sting. But now it had to suffer so many!

Revenge merely increases a problem.

The Golden Goose

Once upon a time there lived an honest farmer who worked very hard. One day he was rewarded for all the work that he had done. A fairy gave him a golden goose.

Every day the goose would lay a golden egg. The farmer would sell the egg, and the money that he got was enough, in fact more to feed his family and to live well. Each day he continued to work, but he did not have to worry about whether he would be able to

feed his family. His wife and children were happy and contented too.

But very soon greed set in. The farmer wanted many more golden eggs and he wanted them all at once. He decided to kill the goose to get all the eggs. He thought that he would become very rich.

And so one day he killed the goose.

What a miserable man he looked when he found no golden eggs inside!

If you covet all you may lose all.

A Fox and a Goat

It was a hot day and so very dry. A fox and a goat were very thirsty. They looked around for a place to quench their thirst.

At long last, they came across a well. But the well had very little water in it. They were so thirsty that they both decided to go down to the bottom of the well to quench their thirst. After having had their fill, the goat panicked about how they would get out of the well.

"Don't worry," said the fox. "You leave that to me. Just help me get out of the well first. All you have to do is stand firm while I climb up with the help of your horns. Once I am out, I'll pull you up after me."

The goat agreed and very soon the fox was out of the well. Once out, it went its way, leaving the poor goat behind.

Look before you leap.

A **Monkey** and a **Dolphin**

A monkey was on board a ship sailing in the sea. The ship had been wrecked by a storm. It was now struggling in the water. A dolphin, mistaking the monkey for a man, offered to take him ashore.

As they were travelling, the dolphin asked the ape whether he was Greek. "Yes," answered the monkey, "I'm from a very well-known family."

"So you must be knowing Piraeus," said the dolphin.

The monkey had tried to outsmart the dolphin and pretend to be a human being, didnot know that Piraeus was the name of a place, and mistook it for the name of a man said that Piraeus was his very good friend.

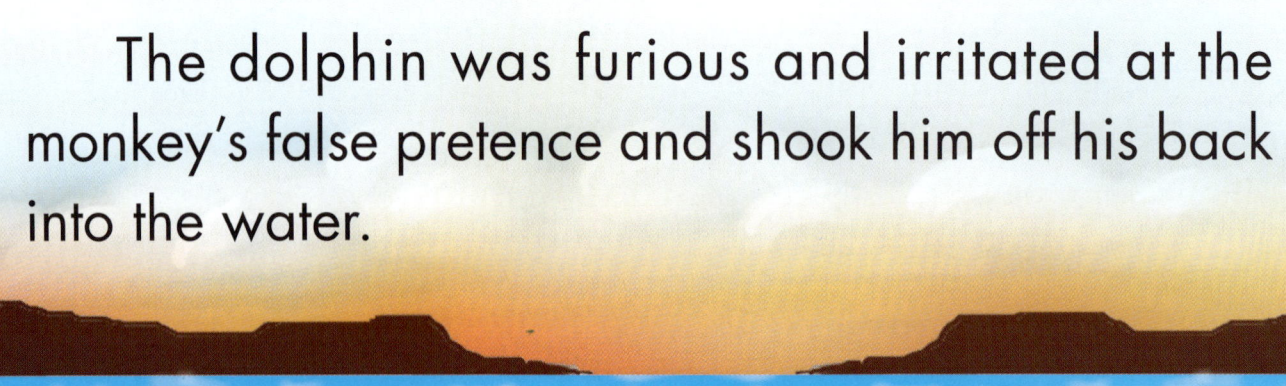

The dolphin was furious and irritated at the monkey's false pretence and shook him off his back into the water.

Who will Bell the Cat?

At the grocer's shop there were mice everywhere. People had started hesitating to come to his shop.

So the grocer kept a cat that chased the mice and always managed to feed on a few. The rest of the time it kept guard and so the mice had no chance to feed on anything anymore.

"We have to get rid of that cat or we'll starve to death," said the mice. But this was not an easy task.

Then one mouse came up with an idea. "Why don't we tie a bell around the cat's neck? Then, whenever she moves, she'll make a noise and that will be a warning for us to hide."

Now came the question of who would bell the cat. They were all scared and held back. Their plan failed.

The Cock and the Jewel

There once lived a cock who loved to scratch about in the grass, looking for tidbits to eat. It so happened that one day, he scratched up a jewel that was so beautiful that it shone brightly in the sunlight.

But it was of no use to him. So he took it to a farmer and got some golden grains in exchange.

An **Ass**, a *Lion* and a **Cock**

A cock and an ass once sat under a tree, sharing a meal. Just then a lion spotted them. "How perfect!" said the lion. "Under the tree sits my meal."

Seeing the lion, the cock began crowing in fear. The strange sound frightened the lion and he fled.

The ass, thinking that the lion was frightened of him, started chasing the lion. The stupid animal did not understand that it was the cock's crowing that had scared the lion. As soon as they were out of earshot, the lion turned upon the ass and tore him to pieces.

A **Fox** and a **Stork**

Once a fox invited a stork to dinner and served it some soup in a flat dish. Though it knew very well that the stork, with its long beak, could not feed from a flat dish, it said, "I hope you're enjoying the tasty meal I prepared."

The stork merely looked on helplessly and so the fox lapped up its share too.

After a few days, the stork invited the fox to dinner and served it food in a jug with a long and narrow neck.

The fox realised that it was being repaid for its behaviour with the stork.

A *Lion* and a *Rabbit*

A lion said to the animals in the forest that if one out of them came to him as his meal for the day, he would not kill any one else among them. The animals agreed to this.

One day it was a rabbit's turn and it took very long reaching the lion. It said that it was stopped by another lion who claimed to be the king of that jungle. "And he wants to meet you, Your Lordship."

"So do I!" said the furious lion.

The rabbit took the lion to a well and showed it its reflection. The lion jumped into the well to chase its opponent and got drowned.

The Two Pots

Two pots floated down the river. One was of brass and the other of clay. The clay pot kept away from the brass pot.

"Fear nothing," said the brass pot. "I'll do you no harm."

"No, no," said the clay pot, "you may not harm me purposely. But if we should happen to knock each other by chance, I'll be ruined. You and I can never do well together."

The Foolish Chicken

There was once a pretty pond with trees around it. A group of ducks went to this pond daily to eat the weeds that grew there.

There was a young chicken who watched them swimming and having fun. It longed to swim like them. But its mother had told it that its feet, wings and feathers were not made for swimming. She warned it not to go near the pond, as it would fall into the water and drown. Yet, wanting to be like the ducks, it dived into the pond, and then it was too late. The poor chicken drowned.

A *Stag* and its Antlers

A young stag was once drinking at a pool. He looked at himself in the water and said, "I have such beautiful antlers, but my legs are so thin!" Just then, the stag heard some hunters coming towards the pool. He fled in fear. His slim legs carried him swiftly away from danger.

Once inside the thick forest, he felt that he was safe. But his antlers, which he loved so much, proved to be his enemy.

They got caught in the branches. No matter how hard he tried, he could not set them free. Very soon the hunters tracked him down and trapped him.

A **Peacock** and a **Crane**

As a peacock and a crane took a walk through the woods, the peacock, very proudly, spread his tail and challenged the crane to show him such a fan of feathers.

The crane paused for a moment and then flew up into the air. He called out to the peacock to follow him if he could.

"You boast about your feathers," said the crane, "which are indeed beautiful, but of what use are they if they do not help you to fly?"

The Dog in a Manger

Once a dog strayed into a cowshed while searching for food. He climbed onto a pile of hay in the manger, hoping to find something to eat. Being hungry, he sat down to eat the hay. But he hated the taste.

The cows soon returned to the cowshed. They were very hungry.

When they went to the manger, they saw the dog there. "Please get off so that we can eat," said one cow.

But the dog refused to move. Even though he could not eat the hay, he refused to let the cows have it.

The **Wolf** in the **Sheepskin**

A cunning wolf was not able to get into a sheep pen however hard it tried. The shepherd kept a careful watch. So one day, it disguised itself as a sheep by wrapping itself in a sheepskin. It crept into the flock and waited for the right moment to catch one for its meal. But the alert shepherd saw the thief among his flock, and hung him up by the same sheepskin, as a spectacle and an example.

115

A Lion and a Bear

Once a lion and a bear, who were quite hungry, happened to find a dead deer at the same time. They fought and they fought. Neither of them wanted to share the meal.

While they were fighting, a fox who had been standing by stole the dead deer and had a good feast.

When the lion and the bear were exhausted,
they found that their meal had disappeared.

A **Dog** and a **Cock**

A dog and a cock took a journey together. At night, the cock rested on the branch of a tree, while the dog slept in a hollow in the trunk.

A fox wanted to have the cock for a meal. He thought of tricking the cock and said that since the cock had such a beautiful voice, he wanted to hug him. The cock said that he could come down if the doorman, who slept in the hollow of the trunk, opened the door to let him out. When the fox went to the hollow, the dog fell upon him.

A Monkey and a Crocodile

Every day, a monkey would eat a mango and give two to a crocodile. Of these, one was for the crocodile's wife. The crocodile's wife thought that since the mangoes were tasty and the monkey ate mangoes every day, his heart would be tasty too.

She asked her husband to invite the monkey home so that she could eat his heart. The crocodile did so reluctantly. But on the way, he told the monkey the reason for the invitation. The monkey said that he had left his heart on the mango tree, and that if the crocodile took him back, he would go and fetch it. As soon as the crocodile took him ashore, the monkey bade the crocodile goodbye!

A *Hunter* and a *Rabbit*

Once upon a time, a hunter caught a rabbit and was carrying it home for his evening meal.

The rabbit was desperate to escape and after trying very hard and being unsuccessful, the rabbit said to the hunter, "If you

let me go, I'll show you where the rest of my companions are hidden, and so your catch will be larger."

The hunter could make out the rabbits plan and smiled to himself.

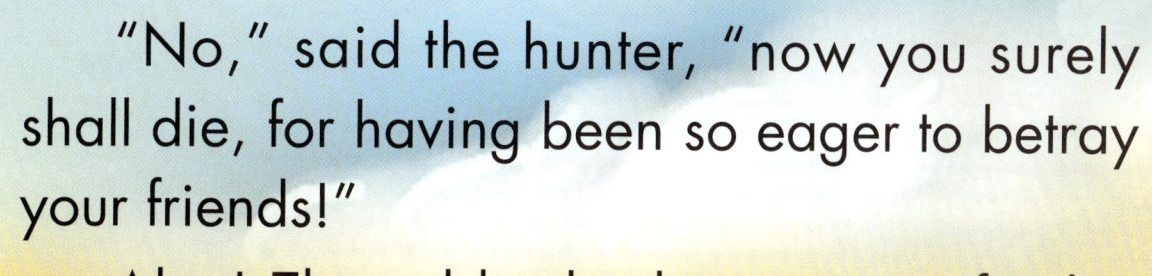

"No," said the hunter, "now you surely shall die, for having been so eager to betray your friends!"

Alas! The rabbit had to give up for his foolhardiness.

The **Lion** going to **War**

The lion was going to war and so he decided to have a meeting with the animals of the forest. Among others, he chose as part of his army, the elephant who would carry his tools of war. He next chose the hare and the ass, but the others wanted them dismissed, considering them to be useless.

But the lion said that each of the animals in his kingdom had a particular talent and that

he found each of them to be of some use. "The ass shall be my trumpeter, to scare the enemy, and the swift-footed hare shall carry my messages home."

A *Young Crab* and her Mother

A mother crab was very worried and anxious because her daughter always walked in a crooked line. No matter how hard she tried, the daughter could not walk straight.

One day, tired and sad, the young crab said, "Mother, I've tried and I've tried, but I can't seem to walk straight. Please, why don't you show me how to do so?"

"Sure, this is how you do it," said the mother, and she too walked a short stretch in a crooked line!

Always practise what you preach!

The **Bee** and the **Bull**

There once lived a bee who was rather conceited. She was quite fussy too. One day, after a long flight, she decided to stop and rest. The place she chose was the horn of a bull that was grazing in a nearby field.

Swooping down, she landed on the bull's horn. Clearing her throat, she asked, "I hope I am not too heavy for you, sir. If so, just tell me and I'll be on my way."

"As you please, little one," said the bull. "But to tell you the truth, I didn't even know that you were there. So I definitely won't notice when you go."

A **Crow** and a **Cockle**

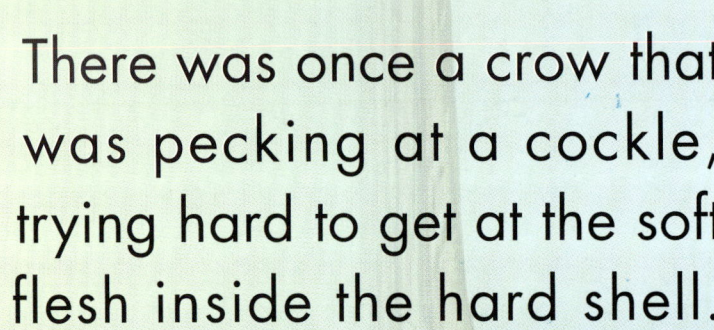

There was once a crow that was pecking at a cockle, trying hard to get at the soft flesh inside the hard shell. Another crow passing by saw its chance of getting the cockle. It told the crow that the best way to break open the shell of the cockle was to drop the cockle from a height. So the crow flew up in the air and threw the

cockle down. The shell broke open.
The other crow was waiting below
and it ate up the cockle.

A **Country Mouse** and a **Town Mouse**

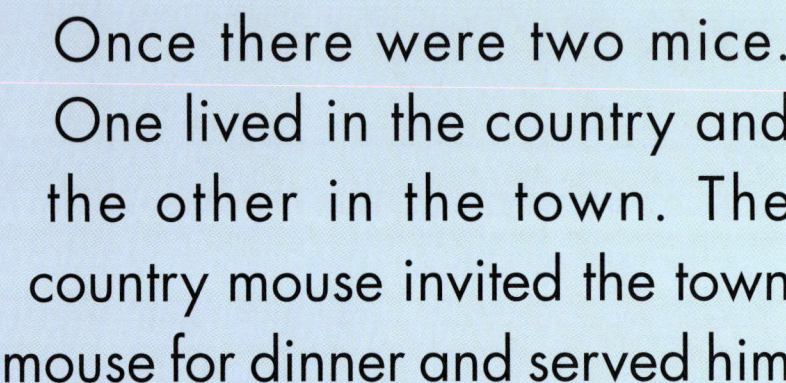

Once there were two mice. One lived in the country and the other in the town. The country mouse invited the town mouse for dinner and served him t h e best food. But the town mouse said that the food was tasteless and invited the country mouse to his house.

At the town mouse's house, the food was very tasty. But all the time, while eating, the town mouse was on the look-out for human beings and the cats they kept to kill mice.

"What a miserable life you lead!" exclaimed the country mouse. "Back, in the country, at least I can eat my meals in peace. Thanks for your hospitality but I think I would like to go back home."

A **Cat** and a **Dog**

A cat sat on the steps of a kitchen looking quite unhappy. Seeing a dog resting under a tree, she went and complained to the dog about the miserly cook who had not given her even a drop of milk since the morning.

"But surely there must be some reason for his behaviour," said the dog.

The cat said that the cook was angry with her because while chasing a mouse, she had knocked down a dish, and since it had smelt very good, she had eaten it all up!

The dog said to the cat, "so now you know the reason for the cook's behaviour?"